W9-CNA-162

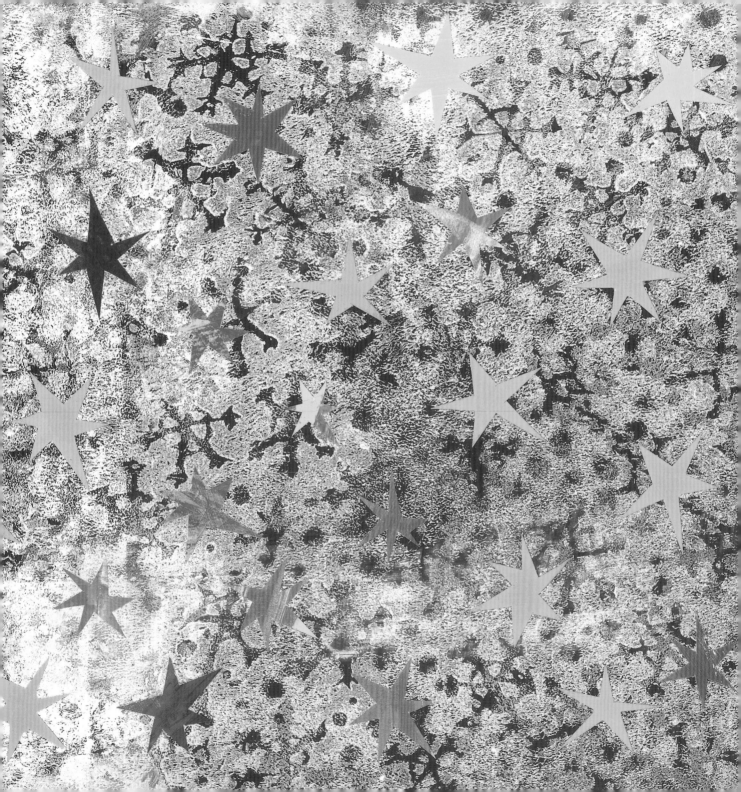

big & SMALL

Original Korean text by Cecil Kim
Illustrations by Petr Horacek
Original Korean edition © Yeowon Media Co. Ltd.

This English edition published by big & SMALL in 2015
by arrangement with Yeowon Media Co. Ltd.
English text edited by Joy Cowley
English edition © big & SMALL 2015

Distributed in the United States and Canada by
Lerner Publishing Group, Inc.
241 First Avenue North
Minneapolis, MN 55401 U.S.A.
www.lernerbooks.com

ISBN: 978-1-925186-51-2

Printed in Korea

Little Moon's Christmas

Written by Cecil Kim
Illustrated by Petr Horacek
Edited by Joy Cowley

It was almost Christmas
and Little Moon was sad.
"No one gives presents to the moon,"
he said to himself.

Little Moon wrote a letter.
"Please, Shooting Star,
will you take this letter
to Santa Claus?"

9

On Christmas Eve,
Little Moon shone on the world.
Then he went to sleep.

He didn't hear the reindeer.
He didn't see Santa Claus.

When he woke up,
he had Christmas presents!
"Oh! Oh!"

What were inside?

Little Moon smiled.
He opened the first present.

What was inside?

15

It was a fine hat!

Little Moon smiled and smiled.
He opened the second present.

What was inside?

It was a book about a teddy bear!

Little Moon smiled and smiled and smiled.
It was time to open the third present.

What was inside?

It was a bouncy ball!

Little Moon opened the fourth present.

What was inside?

It was a Christmas tree!

Little Moon was so happy
he could not stop smiling.
He rolled around the sky.
"Thank you, Santa Claus!"

Some nights,
Little Moon puts on his hat
and reads his book.

Some nights, he plays
with his bouncy ball.

When it is Christmas,
he lights up his tree
to say thank you again
to Santa Claus.